Animal Adventures

A Book of Short Stories

by Dan and Janet Ahearn
illustrated by Peter Fasolino

◆

A Star Named Baxter

Discovered

Oliver lived with his father and his brother, John, in an apartment on the Upper West Side in New York City. When John went to college, Oliver missed his brother very much.

One night, Oliver's father brought home a tiny white puppy. "He'll take a lot of care and love, but he's worth it," he said.

Oliver smiled as he lifted the little puppy. He named him Baxter. Oliver trained Baxter, fed him, and walked him three times a day. He taught Baxter tricks. Oliver had many friends, but Baxter became his best friend. They went everywhere together, even to soccer practice and baseball games.

Oliver was proud of Baxter. Baxter was the most popular dog in the neighborhood. He was smart. He was cute. But he wasn't fancy. His hair was wild and he was often muddy. But his eyes always sparkled.

What really made Baxter stand out, Oliver thought, was the stuff he could do. Sure, he was good at all the usual dog tricks. But Baxter could also pretend to read the newspaper or a book. He

could bring you a toy—and not just any toy but exactly the one you asked for! If you asked him for his bone, he brought you his bone. If you wanted his ball, he brought you his ball! A lot of people thought that Baxter understood English.

No matter how bad your day was going, Baxter made you smile. Baxter acted like he was very happy to be alive.

One morning Oliver was taking Baxter out for his usual walk when a woman came up to them.

She said, "Hi, my name is Sally Rudy. I own Animal Stars Talent Agency. I make little dogs like yours into big celebrities. What's your dog's name?"

When Oliver told her, Baxter jumped straight up in the air. Sally handed Oliver a card and said, "I think that Baxter here could be a star in commercials. If you're interested, have one of your parents call me."

That night Oliver told his father about the talent agent. "It's perfect! Baxter loves being the center of attention," Oliver said, eagerly. So Mr. Barnes agreed to call the talent agent.

Dog in Demand

Everyone at the talent agency loved Baxter. They kept saying how cute he was. Oliver and his father agreed to sign a contract. The agency hired the famous trainer, Percy Perrie, to teach Baxter special tricks. Mr. Perrie and Baxter worked long hours together.

The hard work paid off. Baxter appeared in two commercials and was on a billboard for dog food. His picture was on a dog biscuit box. Oliver was proud of Baxter, but he started to miss him. They were only able to see each other at night.

Baxter's talent agent, Ms. Rudy, took Baxter to the finest hotels and restaurants as publicity stunts to sell dog food. Baxter visited hospitals and appeared at supermarket openings. Baxter and Mr. Perrie even had their own car to take them from place to place. Baxter was becoming a superstar. He couldn't walk down the street without someone asking for his paw print.

The Star Treatment

A few months later, Baxter got a part in a Hollywood movie. Ms. Rudy explained that Baxter would have to be separated from Oliver for three months.

Oliver bragged to his friends at school that his dog was going to be a movie star. But Oliver's heart ached when he thought of being separated from Baxter for three months. Secretly, Oliver began to wish that Baxter weren't quite so famous. But Baxter was under contract, and Oliver had no choice.

Of course, no one asked Baxter how he felt. But he seemed to be upset, too. Even the star treatment he was getting in Hollywood didn't make up for what he was missing. He hardly had any time to play. He couldn't eat his favorite biscuits because Mr. Perrie didn't want him to gain weight. On the set there were people brushing him and perfuming him and fussing over him. The bright lights in the studio hurt his eyes. And to top it all off, he couldn't even snuggle up with Oliver at the end of the day. But no one seemed to notice that he was unhappy.

Out of the Spotlight

One scene of the movie took place in New York, so Baxter came back to town a month later. Oliver went to the set to watch. Baxter saw Oliver, wagged his tail, and started to run to him. Mr. Perrie called, "Stop!" But Baxter kept running. Oliver, his heart breaking, told Baxter to go back to work. So, like the good dog he was, Baxter went back to Mr. Perrie. But his tail drooped and the sparkle was missing from his eyes.

Baxter started to ignore everything Mr. Perrie said. He didn't lift his paw when "Action" was called. He didn't bark. He didn't pretend to read the paper. He just sat there.

First Mr. Perrie was embarrassed. Then he was desperate. He asked Oliver to help him. But even when Oliver pleaded with him, Baxter refused to work. He was on strike.

Oliver took Baxter home that night and tried to find out what the problem was. Baxter sat at the foot of Oliver's bed and looked at Oliver with a sad face. Oliver understood and knew what he had to do.

Oliver took Baxter to the Animal Stars Talent Agency the next morning with his dad. Once he was seated in Ms. Rudy's office, Oliver begged her to let Baxter out of his contract.

"I made a big mistake, Ms. Rudy. Baxter's not happy... and neither am I."

Baxter said "Ruff!" to show that he agreed.

Ms. Rudy didn't want to make a boy and his dog unhappy. She said, "Well, Oliver, an unhappy dog does not make for a happy movie." Baxter was free! Oliver jumped for joy. Baxter jumped around, too.

Soon things went back to normal. Baxter and Oliver spent every possible moment together, just like before. Adoring fans still stopped Baxter on the street. They still wanted his paw print. Baxter always gave it to them. He didn't mind, and neither did Oliver—even though he secretly thought it was silly.

Baxter never went back to show business. He and Oliver had learned what was really important. All the fame in the world doesn't make up for the loss of one true friend.

The Hero With Nine Lives

Chloe lived with her parents and baby brother in the city in a wonderful old house. It stood with other houses in a row on a busy street called Second Avenue. Chloe loved her house. Once the door was closed, she couldn't hear the bustle of the streets. That made her feel very safe.

More than anything in the world, Chloe wanted a cat. She read every magazine and book about cats that she could get her hands on. She collected everything she could find about cats. She even had seven different cat T-shirts.

Then on her birthday, her father took her to the animal shelter. She saw lots of furry kittens. Some were tiger-striped. Some were the color of butterscotch. They were all cute. But then she

spotted a beautiful black cat with little white paws. Chloe's dad was surprised. He thought that Chloe would pick a kitten, not a one-year-old cat. But Chloe said that this cat was just what she'd always wanted.

Chloe picked up the cat and smiled. "She's purring, Dad."

Her father said, "OK, let's give her a home."

The volunteer told Chloe and her father that the cat was unusually brave for such a little one.

"She was saved from some stray dogs that had chased her into the stadium at the college. She's friendly, but she's not afraid of anything. Plus, she's full of energy and likes to play."

Chloe decided to name the little cat "Hero."

When Hero moved into the house, Chloe couldn't have been happier. Each night Hero would snuggle up to her, purring like a little motor.

But there was a problem. Hero behaved well only when Chloe was around. When Chloe was at school, Hero got into trouble. She climbed the curtains in Chloe's room and ripped them to shreds. She knocked over plants. She clawed the couch. She kept going into the linen closet and messing up all the fresh sheets and towels. Chloe couldn't understand it.

Chloe's parents weren't happy at all. Finally, they told Chloe that they had run out of patience. They said that if Hero didn't start to behave, they were going to have to find a new home for her.

That very night Hero gave birth to eight kittens! Chloe was afraid that this would be the last straw. Desperate, she pointed out that Hero was behaving really well now. Hero watched over her family and made sure that each kitten got its fair share of milk. Chloe loved the way Hero moved her kittens around by carrying them gently in her mouth.

"Isn't she great, Mom?" asked Chloe. "Aren't the kittens wonderful?"

Her mother admitted they were cute. But Chloe's mom wouldn't say whether or not the cat family would have to find a new home.

"We'll see," she said.

Hero and the kittens lived in a large box in Chloe's room. One night, at three A.M., Hero let out a loud cry. She started meowing wildly. Her cries woke up everybody in the house.

Chloe's father was angry. He came running into Chloe's room and was about to scold Hero when he suddenly stopped. He realized that the house was on fire!

He told Chloe to follow him as he ran to get the rest of the family. Chloe quickly grabbed Hero and one kitten.

There was no time to pick up the other seven, who were scrambling all over. Chloe was sobbing as she ran out of the burning house with Hero and just one of the kittens.

Fire trucks were already pulling up as Chloe and her family came out to the street. The red flashing lights and sirens frightened Hero, and she began to squirm. Chloe couldn't hold onto both Hero and the kitten. Hero leapt to the ground. Chloe screamed as Hero darted back into the house.

Chloe ran to her father. "We've got to get her!"

"We can't, Chloe. Don't worry. Hero has more sense than to go into a fire. She'll be all right."

"You don't understand!" cried Chloe. "She's trying to save the kittens." And sure enough, soon Hero re-emerged with one of the kittens in her mouth! She dropped the kitten on the sidewalk and ran back into the house. Chloe broke away from her father to follow. She almost made it into the burning house, but a fireman grabbed her just in time. Chloe pleaded with him.

"Please! Help her!"

The fireman took Chloe back to her father. "I'll see if we can find her. But don't you leave your father. It's very dangerous here."

Then he talked to another fireman and the two of them rushed into the house.

These were the worst moments of Chloe's life. She huddled with her family holding the two kittens beneath her coat.

Suddenly, her mother said, "Look, Chloe!"

The firemen had returned with five kittens in their large gloved hands. They brought them over to Chloe.

"But one's missing!" Chloe said. "And where's Hero?"

"We didn't see any others. Now it's too hot to go back."

Chloe started to cry. Then she heard her mother and father gasp. She turned and there was Hero. She was limping and the hair around her ears was singed and smoking. But in her mouth she had the last kitten, safe and sound.

Chloe ran past the firemen. She gently picked up Hero and her kitten, and carried them to her family. Somehow, having Hero and the kittens safe made everything seem a little better.

Chloe's father took off his jacket and made a little nest for the kittens. Chloe carefully placed Hero and the last kitten with the rest of her cats.

An emergency medical technician came over to check the cats. The kittens seemed unhurt. And the medic said the mother cat would be fine, too. Then he asked the cat's name.

"Hero," said Chloe.

"You gave her the right name. She sure saved those kittens."

Chloe's father said, "Not only the kittens! If she hadn't woken us up, I don't know what would have happened. She saved our whole family."

Phineas of the Sea

Ruth woke before dawn and pulled on some old khaki shorts, a T-shirt, and her sneakers. She fastened a chain with a silver whistle around her neck. As the sun rose outside her window, she saw silver glints of light on the gray surface of the Gulf of Mexico. By noon, she knew, the water would be a bright greenish-blue.

Ruth lived with her aunt and uncle on a small island just off the coast of Florida. She spent all her time either near the water or in the water. Her aunt said that Ruth must be half fish with saltwater in her veins.

At the bait shack on the pier, Ruth bought a bucket of fish to use as bait. Then she headed for the cove where she'd first seen the dolphin she had named Phineas, or "Phinny" for short.

Ruth sat on the rocks and scanned the waters of the gulf, waiting patiently.

Suddenly, she saw a black triangle. It appeared for just an instant. If she hadn't expected it, Ruth might have missed it. But she kept her eye on the spot until she saw the fin appear again.

This time the dolphin lifted almost its entire sleek, streamlined body out of the water. It arched and slid back into the sea with a final flip of its tail. Ruth stood up and whistled three times. The dolphin turned toward her.

"Phineas!" Ruth called. "Phineas!" She ran over the sand, seashells crunching underfoot, and grabbed a fish from the bucket. She waded straight out into the water up to her knees. She walked thirty feet out into the cove, then stopped and waited. Soon she saw the dolphin breach the water again just at the entrance to the cove.

"Phineas!" she cried and threw the fish bait high into the air. Before the bait hit the water, Phineas leapt up and caught it in his jaws. Ruth threw fish after fish until the bucket was empty. Then Ruth just stood in the water and watched Phineas cruise back and forth, waiting for more fish.

"Ruthie!" It was her Uncle Ed. He was a fishing guide. He took vacationers out in his small boat to fish and to see the sights. Ed waded out to Ruth, and together they watched Phineas dive and leap. Finally, Ed said, "He's looking for more food."

"No he's not," said Ruth. "He's had plenty. He's just hanging out with me."

"Ruthie, he's a wild creature. He comes for the food." Ed noticed how quiet Ruth became when he said that. So he added, "I don't mean he doesn't care about you, Ruthie. In his way, he does. But the food is very important to him. Too important. You know what I think about your feeding the dolphin, don't you?"

"I know."

"He's becoming dependent on you. He's not hunting now. He hangs around waiting for you to toss him some fish."

"What's wrong with that?"

"He should be with other dolphins. I know you mean well. But we shouldn't interfere with his natural habits. What will he do if you suddenly can't feed him anymore?"

"I'll make sure Phinny always gets fed."

"What'll happen when you go to visit your cousin?" asked Ed.

Ruth looked away.

"Ruthie, you are keeping Phineas from following his instincts. You might even interfere with his breeding and migration patterns."

Ruth bit her lip and didn't answer. She knew that her uncle was right, but she didn't want to lose Phineas.

Ed patted her on the shoulder. "OK, kid. I've got to get to work. I'm going fishing today. Want to come?"

Ruth shook her head. "No thanks, Uncle Ed. I want to stay with Phineas."

Ed looked at Ruth and smiled. He had to admit that what Ruth had with that dolphin was special.

Later that day Ruth and her friends Lisa and Pete went fishing along the banks of the canal at the end of the cove. The kids threw back any fish they caught.

The temperature was 92° and climbing. The three friends were sitting in the shade of a low palm tree. They were drinking bottled water and trying their best to keep cool. Suddenly, Pete jumped to his feet and cried, "Look! Look at that!"

There in the shallow canal was Phineas the dolphin, slowly swimming toward them.

"What's he doing here?" asked Lisa. "I've never heard of a dolphin coming down this canal before. It's too shallow, isn't it?"

"It's much too shallow," said Pete. "Besides, it's so narrow, I don't think the dolphin will be able to turn around."

People living nearby heard the commotion and came out of their homes. A man in a sailor cap called out, "Throw the dolphin a rope." A woman wearing a big white hat yelled, "Call the coast guard." It seemed like everyone had something to say.

Ruth was too shocked to speak. Phineas looked so huge in the small, tight space of the canal. "He's looking for me. He wants me to feed him fish," she said, feeling guilty. "I've got to help him!"

Lisa said, "I don't think he can turn around now. And the tide has gone out. He's trapped!"

People started to panic. They screamed for help.

The three friends ran to Pete's house and called the Florida Fish and Wildlife Office. And shortly after, experts arrived to help Phineas get back to the open sea.

Television news crews also arrived to film the rescue. Newspaper reporters and environmental activists came and wrote things down on notepads. One of them took Ruth aside. She talked to Ruth about the dangers of feeding wildlife.

Ruth tried to listen carefully. But all she could think about was how much she just wanted Phineas to be safe and sound and back in the Gulf of Mexico. If anything ever happened to her friend, she knew that she would never forgive herself.

That evening, as the sun began to set, the rescue teams finally got Phineas back to the cove. Once they got him into the deep water, Phineas swam out to sea.

Ruth watched him go, knowing that she would never see him again. There would be no more buckets of fish. No more whistles. She was sad, but relieved that Phineas was safe.

When she turned away from the water, she looked up at Uncle Ed's face. He smiled at Ruth and patted her on the shoulder.

She would always love her uncle because he did not say, "I told you so."

The Lion

That day they drove for miles and miles across the African plains. Justin Blake was disgusted as he played a hand-held video game. He looked up for a moment. Africa, he thought. Big deal. He went back to playing his game. For about the millionth time, Justin wished that he hadn't had to come halfway around the world to look at a bunch of dust and scrubby little trees.

Justin's father was a photographer for a nature magazine. He traveled by himself to Africa all the time, but this time he had insisted on bringing Justin and his mom along. "You'll like it, Justin," Mr. Blake had said. "It'll get you out of your stuffy room and into the real world." As if this was the real world: no TV, no stores, no movie theaters, no McDonald's. This was the second day of riding around in circles looking for animals for his father to photograph. Yesterday they hadn't seen a thing, and Justin was bored.

Suddenly, the display on his video game screen faded and died. Where would he get batteries? First his laptop had broken and now this! He didn't know much about Africa, but he knew this: There weren't any stores way out here. Maybe they had batteries at the safari inn. He wouldn't be able to stand the boredom without his video game.

Things were so primitive in this country. The Land Rover they were riding in was a piece of junk. And the roads they traveled (when there were roads!) were so bumpy that each jolt rattled Justin's teeth.

Mr. Blake pulled over and stopped the car. He got out and walked away. In the distance, Justin could make out the figure of a running man. He was wearing a red cloth wrapped around his body like a robe and seemed to be carrying a stick. When the man got closer, Justin could see that the stick was really a long spear! The man and Justin's father talked and the man pointed with the spear. Then the man trotted away.

When they were bouncing over the open plains again, Justin asked his father, "Who was that?"

"He's a Masai warrior. His name is Sandoa. He's worked with me before. He tracks big game, like lions. He's found some elephants."

Justin wondered what chance a man on foot had of finding anything in the wilderness, even something as large as an elephant.

"Why doesn't he ride with us?"

"He won't ride in a car. Claims it would make him soft." Mr. Blake looked up at Justin in the rearview mirror and saw a troubled expression on the boy's face. "What's the matter?"

"Oh, nothing. It was just weird seeing that guy appear out of nowhere."

"The Masai are an amazing people. A Masai boy used to have to hunt a lion all by himself before he was considered a man by his tribe. Now the lions are protected, so the Masai have given that up. But imagine facing a lion with nothing but a spear."

Justin sat back and made a face. In the distance he could see the man in the red robe trotting across the plain. It was amazing how far away he was already. Justin thought, What's the use of this one man running around trying to find the elephants? Why not just use an airplane?

After twenty minutes of the bumpiest ride yet, they reached the spot where his father had said they would meet Sandoa. From there they would walk to the elephants. Justin's father got out and started tinkering with his cameras. Justin's mother was just staring around at the barren landscape as if it were the best thing in the world. Justin snorted in disgust and wandered away, kicking little stones. He was so bored and frustrated that he walked without paying attention to where he was going. At home, he was thinking, I could be on the Internet playing real video games or talking to my friends.

Suddenly, Justin realized that he was in a growth of tall, thorny bushes. He couldn't see his parents or the Land Rover anymore. He thought of calling out, but he didn't want his dad to think he was a baby.

That's when he saw the lion. It was standing as still as a statue, and Justin almost wandered right into it. For a moment Justin told himself that's what it was, a statue stuck out here in the middle of nowhere. But it wasn't a statue.

The lion hadn't seen him yet. It was focused on something else. Justin felt sorry for whatever poor creature the lion was watching. But most of all, he was glad that the lion wasn't staring at him. Justin began to back away when he felt a hand on his shoulder. Startled, he looked up into the face of the Masai warrior, Sandoa.

"Be still now, boy. This lion is looking for his lunch. Let him find it."

Sandoa smiled slightly, but he kept his eyes fixed on the lion. Just then the wind changed, and the lion turned and looked at them both.

"If he comes at us, don't run. He'll catch you. Just stand behind me." Sandoa was so calm, so still, so sure of himself, that Justin felt calmer. He gave up any idea of running. It seemed like they waited forever, frozen, trying not to breathe. Then the lion crouched and Sandoa quickly stepped in front of Justin. The lion's tail twitched nervously. Sandoa lifted the spear in both hands. At that moment the lion turned and loped away into the brush.

"Incredible! You just scared him away!"

Sandoa smiled and pointed. "The elephants are coming. Even a lion is afraid of something. Let's go back. We don't want to get in their way, either."

Later, Justin was riding in the back of the Land Rover, watching the sun fall slowly over the African plains. He felt as if his eyes were sharper, as if he could see farther and more clearly than ever before. The land that had seemed so empty to him now seemed full of life. So full that you could never see it all in a lifetime of looking.

When they got back to the safari inn, Justin didn't ask about new batteries for his video game. That night he thought about Sandoa and the lion. When he fell asleep, he dreamed about Africa.